# A Job for Jenny Archer

by Ellen Conford

Illustrated by Diane Palmisciano

Little, Brown and Company
Boston New York Toronto London

Library of Congress Cataloging-in-Publication Data

Conford, Ellen.
A Job for Jenny Archer / by Ellen Conford. — 1st ed.
p. cm.
Summary: Convinced that her family is poor because her parents refuse to get her a horse or a swimming pool, nine-year-old Jenny Archer follows her own path to making money, including a plunge into real estate that puts her house on the market.
HC: ISBN 0-316-15262-5
PB: ISBN 0-316-15349-4
[1. Wealth — Fiction. 2. Moneymaking projects — Fiction. 3. Humorous stories.] I. Title.
PZ7.C7593Po 1988
[E] — dc19 87-24424
CIP
AC

HC: 10 9 8 7 6 5 4 3
PB: 10 9 8 7 6 5

WOR

*Published simultaneously in Canada*
*by Little, Brown & Company (Canada) Limited*

Printed in the United States of America

# A Job for Jenny Archer

# 1

Jenny Archer had money troubles.

"I'm broke," she told her friend Wilson Wynn. "I only have twenty-seven cents to my name."

"What do you want to buy?" Wilson asked.

"I want to buy my mother a fur coat. For her birthday."

"Wow!" said Wilson. "A fur coat must cost at least a million dollars."

"No," said Jenny. "Not a million."

Wilson was her best friend. But he was a year younger than she was and didn't know much about money.

"Even if it costs a hundred dollars," he said, "you can't afford it."

"I know it." Jenny sighed. "I can't afford anything."

"Are you poor?" asked Wilson.

"I guess we must be. Every time I ask my mother to buy me something she says it's too expensive."

Jenny pulled at a curl of her dark brown hair. She twisted it around her finger.

"A fur coat is pretty expensive," Wilson pointed out.

"That's why I want to buy her one," said Jenny. "When she wears it, she won't feel poor."

Wilson knew that Jenny only twisted her hair when she was upset about something. Or when she was thinking hard.

Buying Mrs. Archer a fur coat so she wouldn't feel poor was a great idea, he thought.

Jenny had a lot of great ideas.

But even she couldn't think of a way to buy her mother a fur coat for twenty-seven cents.

Mrs. Archer opened the back door. "Hello, Wilson. Barkley wants to play in the yard. Is that all right with you?"

"Sure," said Jenny. "Wilson isn't afraid of Barkley anymore. Are you, Wilson?"

The big black dog shot out the door. Wilson gulped. Barkley flew down the steps and ran right at him.

He forgot he wasn't afraid of Barkley anymore. He forgot that Barkley loved him. He forgot that all Barkley wanted to do was lick his face.

"YIKES!" he screamed. He threw up his arms as Barkley leaped at him.

"Down, Barkley!" Jenny ordered.

The dog seemed to hang in the air for a moment. Wilson held his breath and squeezed his eyes shut.

When he opened them, Barkley was sitting at his feet, drooling on his sneakers.

"I'm sorry if he scared you again," Jenny said. "He's just glad to see you."

"I wish he wouldn't be so glad," Wilson said. "He's awfully big."

"But he's a good dog," Jenny said. "You know he'd never hurt you. I trained him myself."

That was almost true. Jenny's father had helped. But Jenny had done most of the really hard work herself.

"And you did a great job," said Wilson. "Still —"

"That's it!" Jenny cried. Her eyes lit up. "Wilson, you're a genius!"

"I am?"

"You are." She nodded so hard that her big round glasses slid down her nose. She pushed them back with her finger.

"We're going into the dog-training business," she said.

"What do you mean, *we*?" asked Wilson.

# 2

Jenny woke up at seven o'clock the next morning. It was Saturday. She would have the whole day to work at her dog-training business.

All she needed were some dogs to train.

It was too early to start calling on people, so she sat down and made a list of everybody she knew who had a dog. She counted seven people nearby who owned dogs.

Her mother and father liked to sleep late on weekends, so Jenny made her own breakfast. She took a slice of leftover pizza from the refrigerator. She poured a glass of milk to go with it.

Pizza was her favorite breakfast, besides cold spaghetti and meatballs.

As she ate, Jenny wondered how much money she would make. She wasn't sure what she should charge for training dogs. Maybe she should ask different prices for different kinds of dogs.

If she trained a little dog, she could charge a dollar an hour.

If she trained a big dog, she could charge two dollars an hour.

If she trained a dog not to make a mess in the house, she could charge five dollars an hour.

At eight o'clock she heard Mr. Loomis start to mow his lawn. The power mower roared. Jenny was sure it would wake up everybody on the block.

She gave Phyllis, her giant goldfish, a sprinkle of food. She left a note under her parents' door so they wouldn't worry about her.

Then she went to call for Wilson.

He lived two blocks away. He had a baby brother named Tyler. Tyler started crying at six-thirty every morning. She was sure the Wynns would be awake.

Jenny rang the doorbell twice, as she always did.

"Hi, Wilson," she said when he opened the door. "Time to start our dog-training business."

"I can't." Wilson looked down at his feet. "I have to mow the lawn."

Jenny laughed. "You can't mow the lawn. The mower's too big for you."

"I pick up the grass after it's mowed," he said.

"No, you don't. The bag on the mower picks up the grass."

Wilson chewed on his lower lip. "My father wants me to wash the car."

"Wilson, that's silly," said Jenny. "You're too short to wash a car."

"No, I'm not," he said. "I do the bottom parts."

Jenny started to get angry. "You know what I think? I think you're making this all up. You don't want to help me."

"Listen, Jenny," Wilson said. "You're the dog expert, not me. You're the one who wants to buy a fur coat. Not me. If you need money, I'll lend you my money. But I don't know how to train dogs."

At last Jenny understood. Wilson was still afraid of dogs. Even dogs with good manners, like Barkley.

No wonder he didn't want to help her. She would be training a lot of dogs. A lot of dogs with bad manners.

"That's okay," she said. "It's my job. I'm

the one who should do it. By the way, how much money could you lend me?"

"Three dollars and ten cents," he said. "That's all I've got. But you can have it."

"You're a true friend," Jenny said. "I won't borrow it unless it's a real emergency."

"When is your mother's birthday?" Wilson asked.

"In three weeks," said Jenny.

He shook his head. "I think you're going to have an emergency."

# 3

The first place Jenny tried was only three houses away from Wilson's. Wilson said his parents always complained about the dog that lived there. It was a cocker spaniel named Kiss Kiss. It belonged to Mr. Katz.

It barked all night long.

One night Mr. Wynn got so mad he went over to Mr. Katz's house. He stood in the yard and barked at Mr. Katz for an hour.

Jenny thought that was pretty funny. Mr. Katz didn't.

Wilson's mother didn't think it was funny either. Wilson said she was really embarrassed. For days she peeked through the curtains before she went outside. She wanted to be sure Mr. Katz wouldn't see her.

Jenny started up the steps. She could hear Kiss Kiss barking even before she rang the bell.

"Who is it?" shouted a voice from inside.

"Jenny Archer," she called. "I train dogs."

"Who? I can't hear you!"

"That's because I haven't trained your dog yet!" Jenny shouted.

Mrs. Katz opened the front door. She was a tiny woman. She wore green slacks and a pink pajama top. She didn't open the screen door.

Jenny could see why.

Kiss Kiss was jumping up and running in between the woman's feet. She threw herself against the door. It was as if she wanted to break it down.

She wouldn't stop barking.

"Quiet, Kiss Kiss!" Mrs. Katz screamed.

Finally Mrs. Katz opened the screen door just a crack. She edged her way out. She had to push Kiss Kiss back inside with her foot.

She tried to get her foot out. But Kiss Kiss was too fast for her. He grabbed her fuzzy pink bedroom slipper and tugged it off.

Mrs. Katz leaned back against the screen. She tried to catch her breath.

"Now, little girl. What do you want?"

"I'm a dog trainer," Jenny said. "I can train your dog for you. My price is very low."

Kiss Kiss was still barking and banging against the door.

"I'd be glad to pay you," Mrs. Katz said.

"You would?" Jenny was so excited she wasn't sure she had heard right. She was getting a job at the first place she tried!

"Yes," said Mrs. Katz. "You take that dog and keep it. I'll pay you ten dollars if you promise never to bring it back."

Jenny felt a wave of disappointment wash over her.

"My husband doesn't have to know anything about it," said Mrs. Katz. "It'll be a secret. Just between you and me."

Jenny shook her head. "We already have a dog," she said sadly. "And a fish."

She tried not to think about the ten dollars as she walked down the steps.

Jenny rang doorbells for almost an hour. Nobody would let her train their dog.

Mrs. Serkin said Jenny was too young.

Mr. Kellaway said his dog was too young.

The Parkers said their dog was too old.

Jenny decided that no one believed she could train dogs. They could at least give me a chance, she thought. How do they know I can't do it?

Then Jenny had a brainstorm. Barkley! She would take Barkley with her. Then they would see how well she could train dogs.

Barkley knew how to shake hands. He knew how to roll over and play dead. He knew how to sit up and beg. He even knew how to bring in the newspaper.

Once the customers saw Barkley's tricks, she'd have a hundred dogs to train!

# 4

Barkley followed Jenny down the street. He was so good she didn't even need to use a leash.

Wilson had told her about a new family that had moved in across the street. He thought they had a dog.

"It's up to you, Barkley," Jenny said. "If this doesn't work, I don't know what I'll do."

Jenny walked up to the front door of the green and white house. Barkley stayed right behind her.

She rang the doorbell.

A man in a chef's hat opened the door. He was holding a frying pan in one hand. He had a wooden spoon in the other hand.

Jenny wondered how he had opened the door.

"My name is Jenny Archer," she said. "This is my dog, Barkley."

"It's nice to meet you," the man said. "I'm Ernest Munch and these are my scrambled eggs."

Jenny laughed. Mr. Munch seemed very nice. She hoped Wilson was right. If Mr. Munch had a dog, she was sure he'd let her train it.

"I heard you had a dog," Jenny said.

"We do. Would you like to meet her?"

"Oh, yes," said Jenny. "In fact, that's why I'm here."

"I hope you're not afraid of big dogs," Mr. Munch said.

"No," said Jenny. "Barkley is big and I trained him myself."

"Well, Millicent is a little bigger," said Mr. Munch. "Come, Millicent!"

Jenny heard someone march to the door. It sounded like someone wearing boots.

Four boots.

"This is Millicent," said Mr. Munch.

The biggest dog Jenny had ever seen sat down next to Mr. Munch. The dog looked through the screen door at Jenny and Barkley.

"She's a Great Dane," said Mr. Munch. "She looks scary but she's very gentle. Shall I let her out?"

"I'm not scared," Jenny said. But she began to understand how Wilson felt about Barkley.

"Okay." Mr. Munch opened the screen door and Millicent walked out.

"Sit, Millicent."

Millicent sat down next to Jenny. She was tall enough to rest her head on top of Jenny's head. Even when she was sitting!

"Say hello to the young lady," Mr. Munch commanded.

Millicent held out her paw. Jenny shook it.

Barkley stood up. He made a low, growling noise.

"It's okay, Barkley," Jenny said. "She's a friend. You sit."

Barkley sat. But he started edging closer to Jenny.

"Give the lady a kiss," Mr. Munch said.

Millicent touched Jenny's hand with her nose.

"Would you bring in the paper now?" Mr. Munch said.

Millicent trotted down the driveway. She picked up the newspaper in her mouth. She trotted back up the driveway.

"Would you take the rubber band off it, please?"

Millicent dropped the paper to the ground. She pressed her paw on top of it. Then she worked the rubber band off the newspaper with her teeth.

"Bring the paper to Mommy now," said Mr. Munch.

Millicent picked up the newspaper in her mouth. She pushed the handle of the screen door down with her paw. She walked inside the house.

"Now, what was it you wanted to see me about?" Mr. Munch asked Jenny.

Jenny heard a woman's voice.

"Why, thank you, Millicent. Would you take the baby her bottle?"

"Sorry to bother you," Jenny mumbled. "I must have the wrong house."

# 5

The next Sunday Jenny went over to Wilson's house to return a book she had borrowed.

She rang the doorbell twice. She could hear Tyler crying.

"You're all dressed up," Wilson said when he opened the door.

Jenny was wearing her favorite T-shirt. It had a picture of King Kong on it. She also had on a blue skirt and a string of red beads.

"My aunt and uncle are coming over," Jenny said. "And my cousin Suzy."

She could hear Mr. and Mrs. Wynn trying to calm Tyler down. But Tyler kept on crying.

"Do you have enough money for a fur coat yet?" Wilson asked.

"No," Jenny sighed. "And my mother's birthday is in two weeks."

"Maybe you should get her something smaller than a fur coat."

Jenny nodded. "I know. I decided to get her a fur jacket. That's half the size of a coat. It should be half the price."

Mr. Wynn walked into the living room carrying Tyler. Tyler was still crying. He twisted around in his father's arms. His fists looked like tight little balls.

"Hi, Jenny," said Mr. Wynn. He looked tired.

"Tyler is cranky today, isn't he?" she said.

"He's still teething," said Mr. Wynn. "And I'm getting pretty cranky myself."

"Poor Tyler," Jenny said. "Poor baby."

Tyler suddenly stopped crying. He saw Jenny and reached out with his arms.

"I can only hold you for a minute," Jenny said. Mr. Wynn handed her the baby.

Jenny touched noses with him. "*Boop,*" she said. "*Boop boop.*"

Tyler began to gurgle. He grabbed her beads and began to suck on them.

Jenny loved babies.

"I really have to go home," she said. "I wish I could stay, but my cousin is coming. I have to watch her."

Mr. Wynn lifted the baby from Jenny's arms. Tyler started to wail.

"One of these days you'll be earning money for that," said Mr. Wynn.

"Earning money for what?" asked Jenny.

"For taking care of children. You'd be a great baby-sitter."

A baby-sitter. What a super idea! Jenny wondered why she had never thought of it before.

She was so excited she raced to the door.

"Sorry I have to run," she said. "But I don't want to be late for my first job!"

# 6

The first thing Jenny did when she got home was to make a business card, like the little white cards in the dentist's office. That way Aunt Marian and Uncle Paul would know that she was a real baby-sitter.

She took a piece of paper from her note pad. The pad had JENNY ARCHER printed on it. Next to her name was a little smiling face. She didn't have any small white cards, but she thought the note paper was almost as good.

She pushed her glasses against her nose. She twirled a curl around her finger.

Then she drew an arrow pointing to the smiling face. Under the arrow she wrote:

"THIS IS HOW YOUR CHILD WILL LOOK IF YOU USE JENNY ARCHER'S BABY-SITTING SERVICE. $1.00 AN HOUR. BABIES OUR SPECIALTY."

Then she remembered that Suzy would be her first job. Suzy was two years old.

So she added another line: "TWO-YEAR-OLDS OUR SPECIALTY ALSO."

The doorbell rang. Barkley woofed loudly. There was a great babble of voices from downstairs.

Jenny jumped up. She was about to go and meet the company when she remembered that she hadn't prepared her room. Whenever Suzy came, Jenny put away all her best things.

Once Suzy had pulled the head off one of Jenny's King Kong models. Another time she had colored in Jenny's stamp album.

And she was always trying to feed Phyllis, the fish. Suzy fed her things like popcorn, chocolate milk, and marbles.

But Jenny would be Suzy's baby-sitter today. She wouldn't leave her alone for a minute.

"Jenny!" her father called. "We have company."

"Jenny, Jenny!" Suzy cried. "Company!"

"Coming!"

Jenny grabbed her business card and ran downstairs.

Everybody was standing in the front hall.

Suzy and Barkley were running around in circles. Jenny couldn't tell if Barkley was chasing Suzy, or if Suzy was chasing Barkley.

Suzy yelled and Barkley barked. Jenny's father shouted at Barkley to stop. Uncle Paul shouted at Suzy to stop.

Aunt Marian held her hands over her ears.

Jenny's mother was trying to smile. She

didn't look as if she could keep trying much longer.

Aunt Marian and Uncle Paul kissed and hugged Jenny.

"My goodness," they said, "you're getting to be such a big girl!" They always said that, even though they saw Jenny almost every month.

"You take Suzy upstairs now," Mrs. Archer said. "You can play until dinnertime."

"Okay," said Jenny. She handed her card to Aunt Marian. "This is what I charge for baby-sitting."

Aunt Marian looked surprised. Uncle Paul leaned over to read Jenny's card. He started to laugh.

Jenny's father looked over Uncle Paul's shoulder. He read the card. Then he started to laugh.

Jenny's mother didn't even look at the card. She started to yell.

# 7

"What do you mean?" yelled Jenny's mother. "You want your aunt and uncle to pay you? To play with your own cousin?"

Jenny had never seen her mother so angry. She didn't understand it. What was so terrible about getting paid for baby-sitting?

"I think Jenny's right," said Aunt Marian. "Why should she get stuck with Suzy every time we come? I'm sure there are other things she'd like to do."

Jenny started to feel awful. She didn't really mind taking care of her cousin. She liked children. When she played with Suzy it was almost like having a little sister.

This was just business. She had to earn money for her mother's birthday present.

Now Mrs. Archer looked as though she might never forgive Jenny. Even when she got the fur jacket.

"You don't charge relatives for visiting!" Mrs. Archer scolded.

"I'm not charging them for visiting," Jenny said. "I'm charging them for babysitting."

"And her fee is a real bargain," Uncle Paul said.

"She shouldn't charge a fee!" said Mrs. Archer.

"Maybe she needs the money," said Jenny's father. "Is that it, Jenny?"

Jenny nodded.

"If you needed money you should have asked us," said her mother.

Jenny didn't say a word. What could she say? She couldn't ask her mother for money to buy her birthday present.

"It's a secret," she whispered.

Suddenly Jenny's father said, "Ohhh." He grinned and winked at her.

Maybe he had guessed what her secret was.

"I'll tell you what," he said. "Mom is right. Families do things for each other without charging money. But I think you need money for a really good reason."

Mrs. Archer began to smile. Jenny was glad she wasn't angry anymore. But she hoped she hadn't guessed the secret too.

"Just for today," her father went on, "I will pay you to sit with Suzy."

"Do you think that's businesslike?" Jenny asked.

Everybody laughed. Even Jenny's mother.

Jenny wasn't sure it was right for her father to pay her, but nobody else thought it was right for Aunt Marian and Uncle Paul to pay her.

And she could make a dollar an hour until dinnertime!

"Let's eat very late tonight," Jenny said.

# 8

Jenny and Suzy sat on the floor in Jenny's room.

Jenny decided that being a baby-sitter was very hard work. It was a lot easier just being a cousin.

Being a cousin meant that she only had to play with Suzy a little while. Then they could watch television. But now Jenny felt she should play with Suzy all afternoon. That's what her father was paying her for.

The trouble was that Suzy got bored so fast. And you had to watch her every minute. Suzy could make a great big mess in very little time.

Jenny gave her a small piece of clay.

"Let's make cookies," Jenny said.

Suzy squeezed the clay until it was flat.

"Cookie!" she said. She took a big bite.

"No!" Jenny yelled. Barkley looked up to make sure Jenny wasn't yelling at him.

"No, Suzy! Spit it out! Yuck! Germs! Dirty!"

Suzy made a face and spit the clay onto the floor. Jenny made a face and cleaned it up with a tissue.

Suzy began to cry. "Clean cookie! Clean cookie!"

"Don't cry," Jenny said. She didn't want Aunt Marian to come and help. Taking care of Suzy was Jenny's job.

"I'll get you a cookie," she said.

Barkley lay down next to Suzy. He put his head in her lap.

Suzy stopped crying. "Two cookies," she said.

"Okay, two cookies. Come on downstairs," said Jenny.

Suzy shook her head.

"I stay with Barkley."

"No," Jenny said. "You'd better come with me."

"No! No!" Suzy squeezed her face up. She always did that just before she threw a big temper tantrum.

Jenny didn't know what to do. She was sure she shouldn't leave Suzy alone. But she didn't want her to start screaming.

"Okay, okay," she said. It would only take a minute to get a cookie. And if Barkley kept his head on Suzy's lap she couldn't move.

"Stay right where you are," Jenny said. "And Barkley, you stay too."

KING KONG

Jenny raced downstairs to the kitchen.

The grown-ups were drinking coffee.

"Cookies!" she said. She flew to the bread box. She pulled out a package of chocolate chip cookies.

She raced out of the kitchen and back upstairs.

Just as she got to the top step, Jenny heard a loud crash. It sounded like glass breaking.

"Yay!" Suzy yelled. "Yay, Phyllis!"

"*Oh, no!*" Jenny wailed. "My fish!"

# 9

Jenny ran to her room.

The fishbowl was broken. There were pieces of glass all over the place.

"No, Barkley," Suzy yelled. "Suzy play with fish!"

Phyllis was on the floor. Barkley bumped her out of the room with his nose. He was pushing her down the hall, just as if she were a hockey puck.

"Phyllis!" Jenny screamed.

"What's the matter?" Mrs. Archer called. All the grown-ups started yelling as they ran upstairs.

"Don't move!" cried Jenny. "Watch out for the fish! Stop that dog!"

She grabbed Suzy so she wouldn't step on the broken glass.

The grown-ups were all at the top of the stairs. Barkley couldn't get past them. He turned around and started back toward Jenny. He bumped Phyllis across the floor with his nose some more.

"Barkley, NO!"

He looked at Jenny.

Suzy struggled in her arms. "Suzy go down! Suzy play with Phyllis!"

"Barkley, sit!" Jenny commanded. Barkley was torn. He knew he should obey Jenny. But he wanted to play hockey with Phyllis.

At last he sat down.

Phyllis flopped around on the floor. She looked weak, but she was still alive.

Jenny put Suzy down, then she scooped up Phyllis in her hands. She ran into the bathroom.

"What's going on?" asked Mrs. Archer.

"I have to save Phyllis!" Jenny said. "The tub!"

Mrs. Archer shut the drain in the bathtub. She turned on the cold water. It seemed to take forever to come out of the faucet.

Jenny put her fish in the tub. Phyllis opened her gills a little. She seemed to be having trouble breathing.

She looked dusty.

"Poor Phyllis," Jenny said. "You must have bruises."

For a long minute Phyllis just lay in the water. She didn't move. She didn't try to swim.

"Please, Phyllis," Jenny begged. "Don't die."

She put her hand in the water to make it ripple. Maybe if the water moved Phyllis would move.

Just when Jenny was sure Phyllis was dying, Phyllis began to swish her tail.

"Look!" Jenny shouted.

Phyllis began to glide through the water.

She went slowly at first. Then she began to swim faster and faster around the edge of the bathtub. She looked like an ice skater zooming around a rink.

"Go, Phyllis, go!" Uncle Paul shouted. Everyone started clapping and cheering.

Jenny held her hand against her chest. She could feel her heart pounding. She tried to catch her breath.

This must be the way Phyllis felt, she thought.

Aunt Marian was holding Suzy in her arms. Suzy looked down at the tub. She started to wiggle.

"Suzy take bath with Phyllis! Suzy go in tub too!"

"Oh, no, you don't," scolded Aunt Marian. "You've scared that poor fish enough for one day."

"And you've scared *me* enough for a *week*," said Jenny.

# 10

"I only have three dollars and twenty-seven cents," Jenny told Wilson. "And my mother's birthday is Friday."

They were sitting in front of the TV set in the living room. They weren't paying much attention to it.

"I guess you won't be able to buy her a fur jacket," Wilson said.

"No," said Jenny. "I decided to buy her a fur collar instead."

"How much does a fur collar cost?" Wilson asked.

"I saw one in the paper," Jenny said. "If you lend me your money I only need forty-three dollars."

"*Only* forty-three dollars?" Wilson shook his head. "I think you better forget about the fur collar," he said. "Maybe your mother would like a fur button."

"A button!" said Jenny. "What kind of a birthday present is that?"

"The only kind you can afford," said Wilson.

Jenny twirled her hair around a finger.

She stared at the TV. A man was standing in front of a big car. "I bought this car when I sold my first house," he said.

The picture changed. Now the man was standing in front of a big boat.

"I bought this boat when I sold my second house. Yes," said the man on TV, "I made a million dollars selling real estate. And you can, too!"

"A million dollars," Jenny said.

She sat down on the floor in front of the TV. She didn't move for the next half hour.

When the show was over, her eyes were bright.

"Wilson, I'm going to get my mother a whole fur coat! Not just a jacket. Not just a collar. A whole fur coat. All the way down to here." She pointed at her feet.

"How?" asked Wilson.

"Selling real estate," Jenny said.

# 11

Jenny and Wilson stood outside Marvel's Deli. Jenny held up a sign:

"I think it looks pretty good," she said to Wilson. "You wouldn't think a kid printed it, would you?"

"I wouldn't think so," he said. "But I'm only a kid myself."

"I don't want people to know it's me selling the house," said Jenny. "They might think I'm too young to sell a house."

"They might be right," Wilson said.

They went into the store. There were four customers waiting.

"Hi, Mr. Marvel," said Jenny. "May I put this sign in your window?"

"Sure, Jenny." Mr. Marvel went on slicing salami. "Are you selling something?"

"Our house," she said.

The four customers turned around to look at her. She saw Mrs. Katz and the new neighbor, Mr. Munch. There were two other people she didn't know.

"My niece is getting married," said Mrs. Katz. "They want a house."

"My brother wants to move out of the city," Mr. Munch said. "He's looking for a house near us."

One of the other customers looked at the sign Jenny held. She took a little notebook from her purse. She wrote down Jenny's address.

Mrs. Katz rushed out of the store.

Mr. Munch said, "I'll get the salami later." He ran out of the store after Mrs. Katz.

The woman with the notebook put it back in her purse. Then she followed Mr. Munch out.

"Three buyers and I haven't even put the sign up yet!" Jenny said. "It sure pays to advertise."

"It may pay you," Mr. Marvel grumbled. "But it's costing me all my customers."

* * *

When Jenny got home her mother and father were dressed to go out.

"Where have you been?" her father asked.

"You knew we had to leave at two. Mrs. Butterfield has been here since one-thirty."

Mrs. Butterfield was Jenny's baby-sitter. Jenny didn't think she needed a baby-sitter. After all, she was a sitter herself.

But her parents were too upset for her to argue.

"I just went for a walk with Wilson," she said. "I forgot you had to go to the wedding."

Mrs. Archer hugged her. "As long as you're safe," she said.

"I wish I could go to the wedding," Jenny said. "I love weddings."

"I know," said her mother. "We wish you could come too. But this wedding is only for grown-ups."

"Don't be sad," said Mrs. Butterfield. "We'll have a fine time together."

Suddenly Jenny wasn't sad at all.

She couldn't go to a wedding today.

She had to stay here and sell the house.

# 12

The doorbell rang.

Barkley barked and ran to the door. Jenny ran after him. Mrs. Butterfield followed right behind her.

A man and a woman stood on the front steps. The man was holding a baby.

"We're the Parkers," the woman said. "Is this the house for sale? We'd like to see it."

Mr. Parker looked at Barkley. He held the baby up a little higher.

"I don't know anything about selling a house," said Mrs. Butterfield.

"I do," said Jenny. "I learned how on TV."

"Your parents didn't tell me to show anyone around." Mrs. Butterfield looked worried.

"You don't have to show anyone around," Jenny said. "I'll do it."

"They should have told me," Mrs. Butterfield grumbled. But she let the people come in.

Jenny and Barkley took the Parkers around the first floor. Then they took them upstairs to the bedrooms.

"This is my room," Jenny said. "This would be a good room for your baby."

Jenny thought about the baby sleeping in her room. She thought about not having her room anymore. She thought about not living in her house anymore.

She got a funny feeling in her stomach.

"Where are you moving to?" asked Mrs. Butterfield.

"I don't know," said Jenny. "I didn't think about that."

"If the price is right," said Mr. Parker, "I want to buy the house."

"Do you know how much the house costs?" asked Mrs. Butterfield.

Jenny shook her head. She didn't have any idea what her house should cost.

She was starting to worry about the whole idea.

What if the Parkers bought the house right now? What if her parents came home from the wedding and found they didn't have a home anymore?

She could picture it. Her mother and father would come back tonight. All the furniture would be on the sidewalk. Jenny and Mrs.

Butterfield and Barkley would be sitting on the couch.

In the middle of the front lawn.

"We'll come back tomorrow," said Mr. Parker. "Don't sell the house to anyone else."

"I'll try not to," Jenny said. She really meant it.

Fifteen minutes later the doorbell rang again. It was Mrs. Katz and her niece.

Jenny showed them around the house.

"It would be nice having you live so close to me," said Mrs. Katz. "Look at that nice big window in the living room."

"There's a crack in it," said Jenny. "Right down there near the bottom."

Mrs. Katz's niece looked at the bottom of the window. "It's a very little crack," she said.

Jenny took them upstairs.

"A separate bathroom in the master bedroom!" said Mrs. Katz. "Won't that be handy?"

"My father says he never gets enough hot water up here," said Jenny.

"We could put in a new hot water heater," Mrs. Katz's niece said.

Jenny sighed. It looked like it was going to be harder to un-sell her house than to sell it.

# 13

After Mrs. Katz and her niece left, the doorbell didn't stop ringing. All afternoon Jenny and Barkley showed people the house.

Jenny pointed out everything she could think of that was wrong with the house, but no one paid much attention. Everyone kept saying what a nice home it was.

By six o'clock Jenny was worn out. Mrs. Butterfield looked as if she had been sitting with Suzy for a month.

Even Barkley was tired.

"This is such a surprise to me," said Mrs. Butterfield. "I can't imagine this house without you in it."

"Neither can I," said Jenny unhappily.

The doorbell rang again. Mrs. Butterfield groaned. "More people?" she said.

"I'll get it." Jenny got up and walked slowly to the door. She tried hard to think of some more things that were wrong with the house.

"It's us again!" said Mrs. Katz as Jenny opened the door. "You remember my niece, Barbara?"

A man was standing next to Barbara. "This is my husband, Hal," Barbara said. "Is it all right if we look around again?"

"I guess so," Jenny said.

"Barbara just wouldn't stop talking about your house," the man told Jenny. "She said I had to come and see it before you sold it to someone else."

"Did she tell you about the crack in the window?" asked Jenny.

"What crack?" the man asked.

"Did she tell you about the hot water?" Jenny asked.

"What about the hot water?" the man said.

Both Barbara and Mrs. Katz began to talk at once.

"Now, Hal," said Mrs. Katz.

"Please, honey," said Barbara.

"You didn't say anything about hot water!" the man said loudly.

Barkley began to bark. He hated to hear people argue.

Suddenly Jenny heard the front door slam. Her father and mother marched into the living room.

Mrs. Katz and Barbara and Hal stopped arguing.

They stared at Jenny's parents.

Jenny's parents stared at them.

Mr. Archer held out the sign from Mr. Marvel's window.

"Jenny!" he roared. "Why are you trying to sell our house?"

"To tell you the truth," Jenny said, "I'm trying *not* to."

# 14

It took the Archers a long time to explain to Mrs. Katz and Barbara and Hal that the Archer house was not for sale.

It took Jenny a long time to explain to her parents why she had tried to sell the house in the first place.

"But what made you think we were poor?" her mother asked.

"Every time I ask you for something you say we can't afford it," Jenny said.

Mr. Archer tilted his head to one side. "What was the last thing you asked us for?" he said.

Jenny remembered very well. It was what she wanted more than anything in the world. "A horse," she said.

"Well, we can't afford a horse," said Mr. Archer. "But that doesn't mean we're poor. And do you remember what else you asked us to buy?"

Jenny nodded. It was the thing she wanted second most in the world. "A swimming pool," she said. "With a slide and a diving board."

"You see what I mean?" her father said. "A swimming pool costs thousands and thousands of dollars."

Jenny twirled a strand of hair around her finger. "I get it," she said finally. "It's not that we're poor. It's just that I have very rich ideas."

Her mother laughed so hard she nearly started to cry. She grabbed Jenny and hugged her hard.

"Like fur coats," she said. "Who wants a fur coat? Having you for a daughter is the best present I could get. Even if you do have rich ideas."

Her father took her aside.

"I'm only getting Mom a sweater," he whispered. "If you got her a fur coat I'd look pretty cheap."

He promised to take Jenny shopping Thursday afternoon. He said he would lend her money for a present.

"But then it won't be *my* present," Jenny said.

On Thursday Jenny's father was going to pick her up after school. They would go to the mall. Mr. Archer would buy the sweater.

Jenny would try to find a good present for $3.27.

"You can still borrow my money," Wilson said that morning on the way to school.

"No," said Jenny. "I should buy my mother's present with my own money." She pushed her glasses back on her nose. "It will just have to be a very small present."

She sighed. It was hard for a person with rich ideas to think small.

She could still picture her mother in a brand-new fur coat.

Suddenly Jenny stopped walking.

"Look at that sign!"

# 15

An arrow pointed to a red house on the corner.

Jenny ran toward the house. The garage door was open.

The garage was filled with all kinds of things. Clothes and games and tools. Dishes and pots and old records.

"I bet I can find a present here," Jenny said.

A woman in jeans was sticking price tags on some cups.

"The sale doesn't start until ten," she told Jenny.

"But I'll be in school at ten," said Jenny. "And my mother's birthday is tomorrow."

The woman smiled. "Well, I guess you can look around. Since it's for your mother."

"We'll be late for school," Wilson said.

"You go ahead," Jenny said. "I just know I'm going to find a present here."

But Wilson stayed. "Jenny, look!" He pointed to a table piled with jewelry and belts.

"You wanted to buy your mother a fur collar. There's a collar."

Jenny picked it up. It wasn't fur, but it was beautiful. It looked like the collar of a shirt.

75¢
2.25
1.50
2.00
75¢
95¢
$1.00
$2.00
$1.50
2.50
3.00

Only it was very soft and creamy colored. Jenny could see right through it.

"Isn't that pretty?" the woman said. "It's lace."

"Would it go with a sweater?" Jenny asked.

"Yes, you could wear it with a sweater."

"It's perfect." Jenny sighed. She was afraid to ask how much it cost.

"I was going to sell it for six dollars," the woman said. "That's a very good price."

"Oh." Jenny looked down at her sneakers. She hoped she wouldn't cry.

"I can lend you money," Wilson whispered loudly.

Jenny shook her head.

"How much money do you have?" the woman asked.

"Three dollars and twenty-seven cents," said Jenny. "My father would lend me some. But I wanted to buy the present by myself."

"I understand," said the woman. "If you were my daughter I'd be proud of you."

"Thank you," said Jenny. But she didn't feel very proud.

"I'll sell you the collar for three dollars," the woman said.

"You will?" Jenny couldn't believe her ears. "Really?"

She grabbed Wilson and started jumping up and down.

The woman picked up a white box and a package of blue wrapping paper.

"I'll sell you these for twenty-five cents," she said.

"That's just right!" Jenny cried. "I even have two cents left over!"

Jenny thanked the woman again and again.

She took $3.25 from her red purse. She was so excited she dropped a nickel.

The woman put the collar in the box. She

put the box and the blue paper in a small bag.

Jenny and Wilson ran the rest of the way to school.

The crossing guard made them wait on the sidewalk.

"Oh, Wilson!" Jenny hugged the paper bag to her chest. "I can't believe it," she said. "It's the perfect birthday present. And you found it!"

She peeked into the bag. She opened the white box.

"It's so beautiful," she said. "My mother will love it."

"I hope so," said Wilson. "Because you only have two cents left in the world. Now you're really poor."

"No, I'm not," Jenny said. "I was just trying to get too rich."

They crossed the street. They ran up the school steps.

"I'm glad you're not poor," said Wilson. "You won't have to borrow my money."

"My father's birthday is in July," said Jenny as they walked down the hall to their classrooms.

"Uh, oh," said Wilson.

"Don't worry," Jenny said. "I learned my lesson. I know I can only buy him a small present."

"A very small present," said Wilson. "A two-cent present."

Jenny pushed her glasses back on her nose. Her eyes were shining.

"That's right," she said. "But I'm going to give him the biggest birthday party you ever saw!"